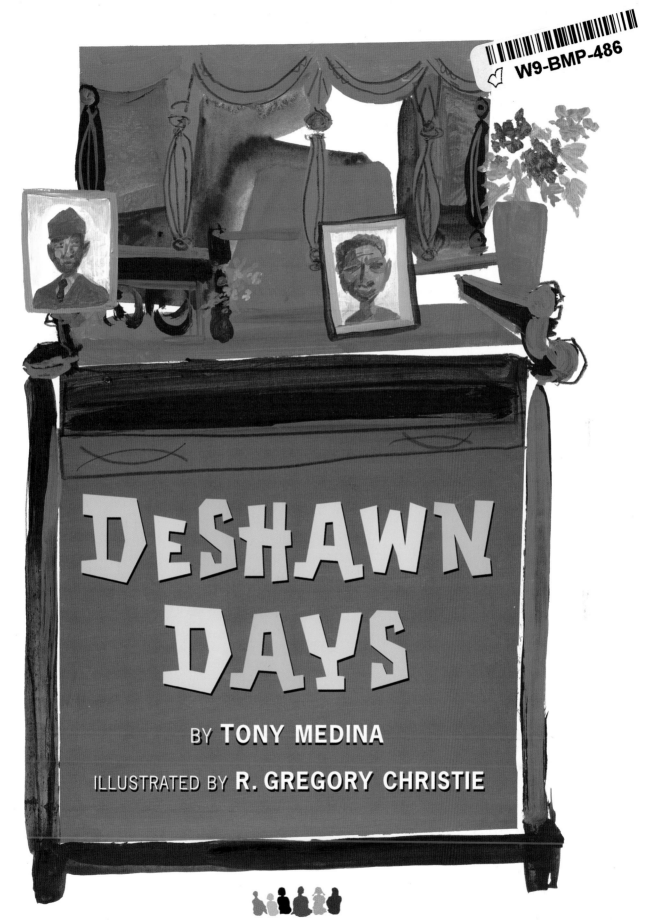

DeSHAWN DAYS

BY **TONY** MEDINA

ILLUSTRATED BY **R. GREGORY CHRISTIE**

LEE & LOW BOOKS INC. • **NEW YORK**

To the women in my life, my three aunts:
Vilma, Rachel, and Josie.
And to the memory of my grandmother,
protector and friend, Augusta Medina—T.M.

For D.—R.G.C.

Text copyright © 2001 by Tony Medina
Illustrations copyright © 2001 by R. Gregory Christie
All rights reserved. No part of the contents of this book may be
reproduced by any means without the written permission of the publisher.
LEE & LOW BOOKS Inc., 95 Madison Avenue, New York, NY 10016
leeandlow.com

Manufactured in China by South China Printing Co., March 2013

Book design by Christy Hale
Book production by The Kids at Our House
The text is set in News Gothic
The illustrations are rendered in acrylic

(HC) 10 9 8 7 6 5 4 3
(PB) 15 14 13 12 11 10 9 8 7 6
First Edition

Library of Congress Cataloging-in-Publication Data
Medina, Tony.
DeShawn days / by Tony Medina ; illustrated by R. Gregory Christie.—1st ed.
p. cm.
ISBN: 978-1-58430-022-9 (hardcover)   ISBN: 978-1-58430-228-5 (paperback)
1. Afro-American boys—Juvenile poetry. 2. Afro-American families—Juvenile poetry.
3. Inner cities—Juvenile poetry. 4. Children's poetry, American. [1. Inner cities—
Poetry. 2. Afro-Americans—Poetry. 3. Family life—Poetry.] I. Christie, R. Gregory,
1971- ill. II. Title.
PS3563.E2414 D4 2001
811'.54—dc21   00-061936

Find out more at leeandlow.com/books

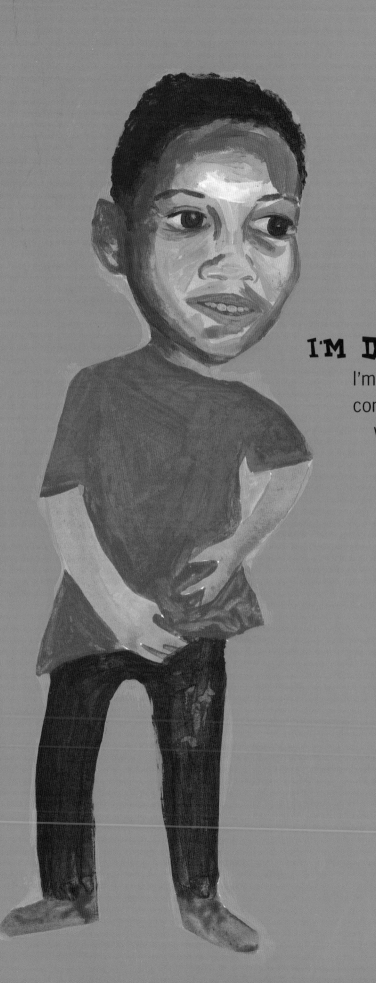

I'm DeShawn Williams

I'm ten years old
come see who I live with—
who I love!

IN MY HOUSE

My uncle my uncle
he lives in my house

And my mother of course
who's hardly ever home
'cause she works so hard
and goes to college too

A lot of people live here—
my cousin Tiffany
and her mother too
with the TV always on
and people talking loud
laughing at funny jokes

My grandma my grandma
she lives in my house

Praying or cooking
with me under the table
listening to the grown-ups
telling stories and the kitchen
is warm and the windows wet
with the smell of cornbread
and baked chicken

My mother my mother
she lives in my house

Working hard all day 'cause
she don't know where
my dad is at
coming home from work
and school real tired
and me running to the door
with a big hug and kiss
helping her put her books away

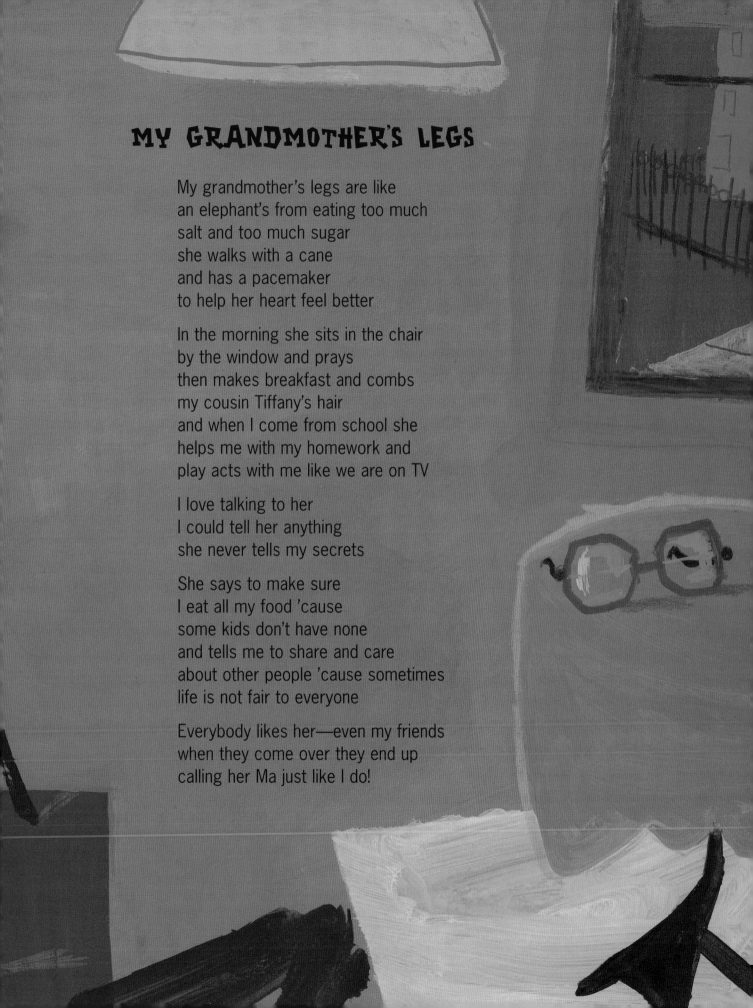

MY GRANDMOTHER'S LEGS

My grandmother's legs are like
an elephant's from eating too much
salt and too much sugar
she walks with a cane
and has a pacemaker
to help her heart feel better

In the morning she sits in the chair
by the window and prays
then makes breakfast and combs
my cousin Tiffany's hair
and when I come from school she
helps me with my homework and
play acts with me like we are on TV

I love talking to her
I could tell her anything
she never tells my secrets

She says to make sure
I eat all my food 'cause
some kids don't have none
and tells me to share and care
about other people 'cause sometimes
life is not fair to everyone

Everybody likes her—even my friends
when they come over they end up
calling her Ma just like I do!

WHAT IS LIFE LIKE IN THE 'HOOD

You don't just hear music
you hear sirens too
cop cars and ambulances
screaming all the time
real loud at you

What is life like in the 'hood

People walking everywhere
broken bottles in the stairs
crooked spray paint letters
on benches and buildings
and dog mess smell in the air

What is life like in the 'hood

In the summertime
everyone hangs out
in front of the building
playing cards and dominoes
and me and my cousin Tiffany
put on a show—and she thinks
she's a magician doing rabbit tricks
with a hamster and I'm
saying corny jokes and
making funny voices
like a comedian

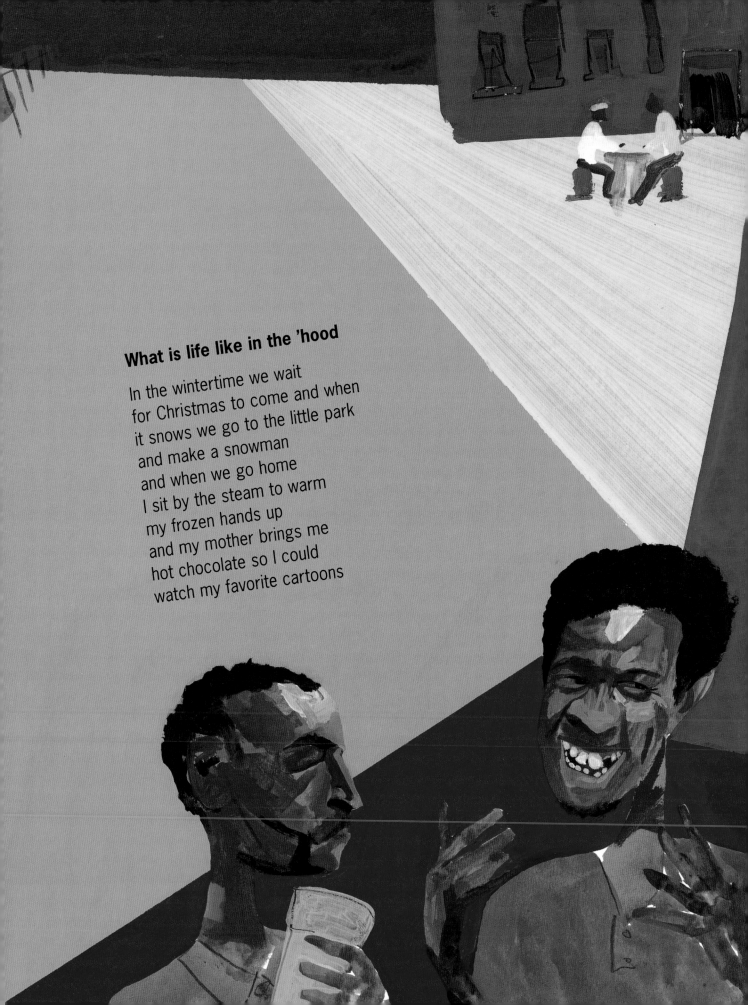

What is life like in the 'hood

In the wintertime we wait
for Christmas to come and when
it snows we go to the little park
and make a snowman
and when we go home
I sit by the steam to warm
my frozen hands up
and my mother brings me
hot chocolate so I could
watch my favorite cartoons

MY COUSIN TIFFANY

My cousin Tiffany
she's ten too
and tall and tough

When we was littler
we used to fight
all the time

But she would always
beat me up
'cause she was tougher
and stronger

I used to say
it was because she
was a girl
and I didn't want
to hurt her

And she asked me
do I think
girls are weaker
than boys

I thought
and thought
for a real long time
but couldn't answer
her back

Besides
she was
sitting on me
at the time!

WATCHING THE NEWS

I used to think watching the news was boring
the only thing I watched on TV was
cartoon videos and comedy shows

Now our teacher makes us watch the news
she says we need to know what's
going on in the world

When I watch the news it's always
about somebody dying and there's
always mothers and kids crying
because somebody got shot or
two countries are fighting

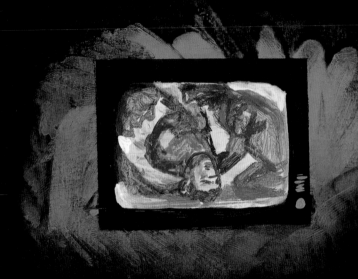

When me and my friends fight
it's just for play
when somebody starts with me
I tell the teacher
or we just fight and that's it

But when big people fight—in a war
they use bombs and rifles and machine guns
like in the movies
they blow everything up and people are
left without a place to live

And it makes me sad to see kids and
their mothers crying because of war

That's why we shouldn't fight

I used to think watching the news was boring
but now I think it's scary too!

MY FRIEND IN SCHOOL

My friend in school
is Johnny Tse
you say it like
the letter C
he's Chinese
I like that 'cause I learn
new things from him
like different foods to eat
new words to speak
and—oh yeah—
                    karate!
which is Japanese—not Chinese
and I don't like it too much
'cause you gotta kick real high
but I like the clothes
you have to wear

I go over to his house
to play video games
he comes over to my house
to eat and to watch cartoons

My friend in school
is Johnny Tse
which sounds like C
or see or sea
or sí (that's Spanish
if you didn't know)

My friend in school
is Johnny Tse
he's Chinese
and likes to sneeze
and when he does that
in school or outside
we laugh and laugh
and people wonder what
and wonder why and
what's so funny all the time

I HATE GRAFFITI

I had a dream that I was
by the handball court
in the park and the scary
tangly black marker
words grabbed me and
tried to stick me to the wall
but I got loose and ran
and then the graffiti from
the park benches started
chasing me
so I ran into my building
but couldn't take the elevator
'cause there was graffiti there too
I went into the staircase but the walls
had black marker scribbles
everywhere and they were all
laughing at me
I was so scared I began to cry

Then my uncle Richie
came and all the tangly letters
and words and names went back
to their walls and benches

He hugged me and
kissed me and said

Don't worry DeShawn
it's just words
they can't hurt you

And then I woke up
to write it down in my book

I used a black marker!

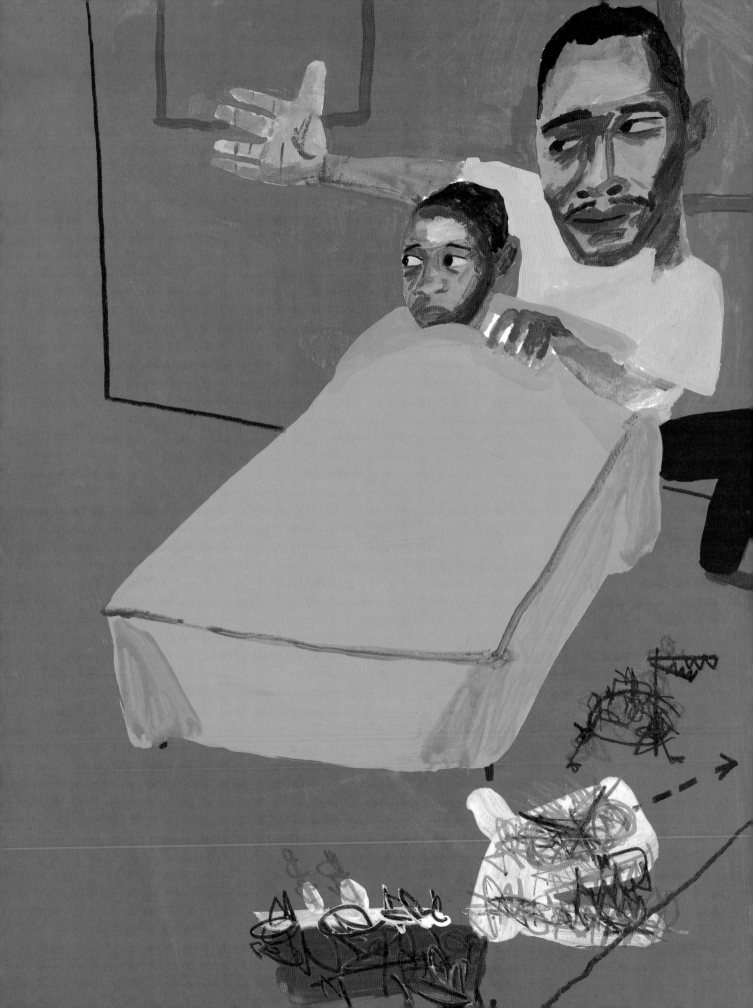

I LOVE RAP

I love rap
not just 'cause of the beats
that make you move your feet
but the words
'cause they talk about reality
'cause they talk about me
and my block

I love rap and I love rhyming
and sometimes I be timing
Tiffany when she's on the mike
and I'm the deejay wavin' my hands
in the air scratchin' make-believe records

But I'm not lesser 'cause I use
the top of my mother's dresser
'cause

I love rap
and I love rhyming
in front of the mirror
making believe I'm in a video
wearing a baseball cap
and my uncle's shades
and when I let my hair grow out
I'll have me some braids
and when I get older and bolder
I'll learn how to break dance
with my legs in the air
kicking like propellers
standing on my hands
bustin' out rhymes
with Tiff and the fellas

STAYING UP LATE

My grandma lets me
sleep with her

When I'm too scared
of the dark because

I had a bad dream from
watching scary movies

Or when I can't breathe
'cause of my asthma

She rubs medicine
on my chest

And leaves the light on
so I can sleep

But instead I stay up
with her watching TV

While she does her
crossword puzzles

Then I fall asleep and
dream good dreams

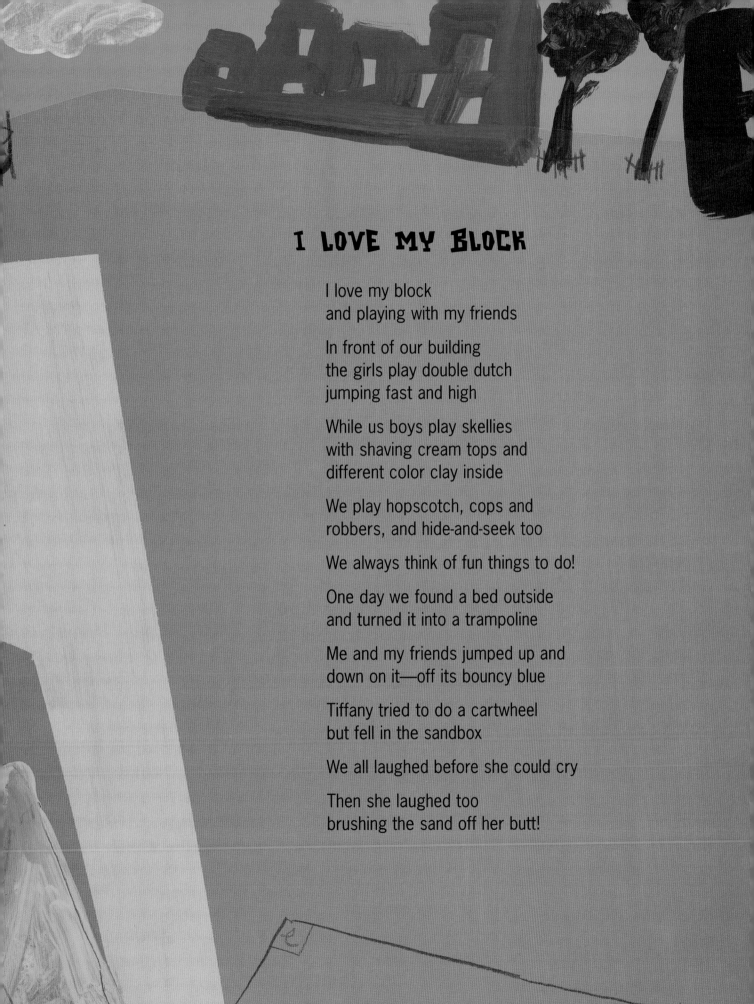

I LOVE MY BLOCK

I love my block
and playing with my friends

In front of our building
the girls play double dutch
jumping fast and high

While us boys play skellies
with shaving cream tops and
different color clay inside

We play hopscotch, cops and
robbers, and hide-and-seek too

We always think of fun things to do!

One day we found a bed outside
and turned it into a trampoline

Me and my friends jumped up and
down on it—off its bouncy blue

Tiffany tried to do a cartwheel
but fell in the sandbox

We all laughed before she could cry

Then she laughed too
brushing the sand off her butt!

CHEERING PEOPLE UP

I was feeling sorry
for those kids
that I saw in the news
who were bombed
in the war

So I told my teacher
that I wanted
to write them a letter
to make friends with them
and cheer them up

Like when Miss Feagan
our first grade teacher
was sick in the hospital
because she had a baby

And she said it was
a good idea and then
the whole class
got to write letters
to the kids in the war

Even though we didn't
get letters back
I still think
we made friends

WHEN MY GRANDMOTHER DIED

When my grandmother died
I cried and cried
until I couldn't
open my eyes

She was the whole world
to me
big and round
and all full
of hugs

She was my favorite

When my grandmother died
I didn't want it
to be sunny no more
because nothing was funny
no more

She was my everything
my protector and friend
she didn't let nobody
pick on me
and always had
nice things to say
even when she didn't
feel good that day

When my grandmother died
I cried and cried

IN MY MOTHER'S ARMS

At school I didn't cry
about missing
my grandmother

Instead I asked
my teacher
what happens
when you die

She said she thinks
we go off to be with
the angels

To do good things
for other people

Answering wishes
and helping them make
their dreams come true

After school my mom
was home waiting

She held me in her arms
and didn't let go
for a long long time

MY PRINCESS STORY

Once there was a princess
she was ten years old like me
and she lived on my block
in the big building across the street

She was trying to go to school
but these other kids who were bullies
followed her
calling her names and bothering her

Then there was a hero
he looked like me
he was wearing a cape
and could fly high

Higher than the tallest tree
and the biggest building
in the projects in my
neighborhood

He ran after the bullies and chased them
away then came back and picked
up the princess with one arm
and flew her to school

She was safe and could do her work
she went to school on time and
the teacher wasn't mad

Then the princess thanked me by
kissing me on the cheek
and I turned red because
I was embarrassed

The whole class laughed
and the teacher too
and we all lived happily
ever after

The end

AFTERWORD

I come from a similar world as DeShawn. I was a skinny brown boy from the projects with asthma, an active imagination, and a grandmother who was there for me. She was always laughing at my antics and teaching me right from wrong, to be patient, and to care about others, not just myself. I had a lively sense of humor that was encouraged by family, friends, and TV. My imagination was always running wild. Every other day I wanted to be something different: a construction worker, a sailor, a movie star, a comedian, a lawyer, you name it!

It wasn't until I was in the ninth grade and I read a book called *Flowers for Algernon* by Daniel Keyes that I fell in love with reading. The book was on a reading list for a class assignment, and something about the title intrigued me. I read it in a few days. It was the first book I ever finished. When I was done a light bulb went off in my head—reading was like watching TV! Only it was my own personal TV because my imagination added to the story. I was the only one to picture the story that particular way. With TV, everyone sees the same thing. But a book is different. I thought, what an incredible thing a writer can do, to create an entire world from one's imagination. I wanted to do that, too. From that day on I wanted to be a writer, and I went on to read everything I could get my hands on.

A writer is a great thing to be because you get to paint pictures, tell stories, create worlds, and express your feelings—all with words. It just takes imagination. DeShawn uses his imagination to see things differently and to help others. Maybe his experiences will inspire you to write poems, paint pictures, sing songs, or help others, too!

—Tony Medina